CAT MOTHER

A Picture Book with a Magical Story

Lili White

ISBN: 979-8-218-07691-7

She didn't know if it was summer or winter, day or night.

The sky leaked out

of a shack it shared

with a pond that sometimes

would suck itself smaller

and drain into a space

> *as big as*

> *a cereal bowl.*

There the globalettes swam for two years or so.

The Link

GENI FOUND a small stone lying in the built-in tray of her aunt's bureau drawer that she had inherited. This stone was indistinguishable from any other. What had it meant to her aunt? Saved sometime in a time zone spanning seventy years before; it must have evoked important memories.

Geni climbed into bed. Durante jumped in beside her. Cats are definitely better than people. Graceful acrobatic dancers—they don't need to be taken out for walks, or given baths. Although cats made her sneeze, Geni's inhaler would never fail to bring back the status quo of normalcy. She couldn't, wouldn't live without her cat.

A SouthWest travel book seemed to concur: A 2000-year-old puma carved into a rock panel. "Look at it hiss," Geni emoted, holding up the picture to Durarte. "IT's YOU!!!!" The cat raised its chin into the air and sniffed gingerly. He never hissed.

Yeah, cats are definitely better than people. Except for Tom, her husband, who was now gone. Covid did that. Geni loved Tom. He did everything for her. He left a big hole behind that would never get filled.

Geni thumbed through the book's pictures of ancient ruins in pristine lands. She loved the West, the sensation that sandstone brought beneath her feet and the smell of the desert air.

Geni had visited the SouthWest with Tom—only him, no one else. Now that would be different. Her husband was dead. She was grateful her old friend Amy would accompany her this year. It would feel good to get out there and break the tension brought on when thinking about the past.

The trip needed a lot of planning, so not a moment could be wasted. Many sites had "permission" requirements. Specific dates had to be registered in advance. She planned it all out.

To the cat she remarked, "I'm going to jump on those rocks, just like you jump."

She slept, and dreamed. By the next afternoon the cat would be dead.

A Dream

GENI CLIMBED two stories of a wide white marble staircase.
A man in Arab costume accosted her, attempting to pull her away with him into his sheets. She resisted. An older man with a full white beard sat on the steps and remarked, "Don't worry, he won't hurt you." They were the only ones there. She ran past them up the stairs to arrive inside a dark palatial room with several doorways. Indiscernible figure paintings encased in heavy gold baroque frames saloned themselves on the walls.

Near the back, on the far side of the room, a family stood enshadowed: father, tween boy, teen girl, and a mother who murmured:
"I don't know what happened, it fell out yesterday I have to find it . . . if we find it everything will be alright."

Tables placed here and there clutched bunches of tangled jewelry. The floor held scattered heaps of the same muchness. Geni reached through the knotted metal chains and gently shook them to see if anything would drop out. She got down on her hands and knees and crawled across the floor from clump to clump looking for loose pieces.

A man in a suit entered a door frame near her. The light behind rendered him in silhouette. Geni turned back and looked up at him. He looked like an old TV actor—what was his name? "It's not here," she said. He responded, "I know about that." The family disappeared. He walked out.

Overwhelmed, Geni's head fuzzed up. Two black clouds grew, hovering around her brain & navel. Their soft black tentacles secretly connected to love lost long ago. They nestled into a hollow space inside where they dwelt in rest or agitation. Geni's asthma kicked in; she woke up coughing. She retreated to the adjoining room to find her mermaid sequined backpack. It sparkled a light in the inky room. Buried inside: her inhaler. She sucked it.
The taste of salt, the taste of salt in the mouth.
Now restless, she knew there was nothing she could do. Her hunger could not be fed. She was privileged: unlike people living in camps without home or country to shelter them. She could sleep safe, unharmed. Except she couldn't. Connections perceived, personal or universal, invaded her.

Geni looked at the objects encased in her grandmother's china cabinet. Memories snapped: attaching each piece to shifting tones of time: the puppet Uncle Jeff made, Yuki's wood card, the gold vase from her grandparents' wedding anniversery . . . her eyes snagged on the vintage, 1-inch tall, paper salt cellar labeled PERSONAL SALT. The company's slogan had been, "When it rains, it pours." Yes, it was raining in her heart.

Everyone, everything, welled feelings submurged forever, surged upwards: guilt, sadness, joy. Shapes and colors registered deep impressions connected to the lost. Touching the bric-a-brac brought calm. Her little collection of beauty equalized the traps, bruises, breaks, and kinks that entered from the outside world. Lifting her up, they surrounded her in serenity and helped define her to herself. After a glass of water, she returned to bed.
In the brightness of morning, her cat was sick.

Motel Utah

IN AN OLD MOTEL in Utah the rattling din of hail on the roof woke Geni. Amy, asleep in the next bed, wore a medical boot on her left foot. Geni leapt out of bed and looked out the window. Lightning flared. Torrents of rain flooded the roads. She registered the hurricaned streets from the motel balcony with her phone, as the shifting mermaid sequins on her backpack presented its own thunder glyph.

Back inside, Amy was up and looking out the window: "I thought they said there was a drought, there must be two feet of water out there." Geni slithered along the spaces between bed, bath, and sink; her cell phoned the park's rangers as she asthmatically coughed. Connected, she stressed, "Hi! I'm on the list to visit the ruin today, but I'm trapped in my motel because of this weather. It's hailing here, is it possible to come tomorrow?" She used her inhaler. "We came all the way out here just to see it."

They got permission to see the ruin the next day. They watched the weather reports play on the TV all day long, heated up food in the microwave, straightened up their luggage, and made drawings with animal stencils.

Geni told Amy, "This trip will definitely lift me out of my depression, or at least set me on a new path. I'm so glad you came."

Amy agreed, "Me two! My foot doesn't really bother me. Hanging around here is boring, but tomorrow'll be fun." Geni replied, "I'll be MORE than disappointed if we don't make it to the ruin; that's the main reason why I came."

She reached for a stencil. A stinging magnetic energy pulled her hand to the puma. *BIZARRE!* She shook her hand off and looked to see if Amy had noticed anything. Amy was oblivious. She stood tall and fully composed. She was combing her hair. Geni relaxed and let go. She colored the puma shape purple. She felt a spirit buzz through her soul, in an electrical kind of way.

Then she caught a reflection in the mirror. It was an American Amandapuss, a feminine face, almost human, half-way cat. She was clothed in a fuzzy white cat-suit with multi-colored horizontal stripes. A sheer acetate scarf with matching stripes and gold threads, was tied up around her head. Geni had no idea how she could see this creature, let alone know its name, given that it was invisible to Amy.

Geni did not share this discovery with Amy, as she couldn't trust how Amy would handle it—jealousy, just plain weird, whatever. She couldn't be saddled with additional negativity. She just didn't have the energy to deal with that.

White Rock Leap

THE RANGERS said there was just one way to the ruin.
Find the white bolder, hop onto the trail beneath it and descend
to the bottom of the canyon. Climb the next mesa. The site was
tucked up top, underneath its lip.

Amy registered fear as she and Geni look over the edge of canyon.
"Are they all like this?" It was exceptionally steep, and even Geni
was a little scared. "No, this is like nothing I've ever seen."

Amy looked at her foot encased in a black boot. "I wish I could go,
but . . ." She caught an odor: "Do you smell that? It smells like cat
scent." Geni was distracted by the height but managed to answer.
"Oh, yeah, I guess there could be a big cat around here; like a
mountain lion, you know, a puma," She paused, "Well, no use
standing around," and off she went.
Amy looked at her watch: 1 PM. "I'll wait right here. Be careful."

Geni shimmied onto the switchback course—it was a sheer drop.
She reached the big white rock, about seven feet cubed. She climbed
onto the top and explored how she'd jump. The rock hung off the
side of the canyon at a precipitous angle. She had to jump—it was the
only way to the site and that is why she came here. There was only
one way down and one way back. But upon her return, how would
she get back up onto the white bolder? She set aside that thought and
concentrated on her jump.

She maneuvered this way and that, attempting to get over this hurdle.
If she didn't land flat on her foot, just so, she could be injured or even
fall to her death. She held on to the sides of the rock and attempted
to lower herself down to lessen the drop. She tried this move using the
front, then the back of her body, but it wasn't going to work.
She got off, walked around the rock, and sat down on the ground, to see
if she could crawl down to the path below. But the shape of the rock,
along with the angle of the eroded ground supporting it, prevented that.
She stopped. She went back to the top of the rock, and contemplated
how she could make it as the wind rushed by her ears.

The Amandapuss entered. She sat cat-like next to Geni who didn't
see her. Today, her headband matched her fuzzy white shirt with
multicolored stripes, that sloped off her shoulders. It helped keep the
wind out of her ears. She glanced at Geni, "Well, have you decided?
What exactly are you going to do?'

Geni could sense the pressure the Amandapuss brought to bear.
She grew more frustrated. Considering her attempts at chancing the
jump, she calculated only people taller than five foot five could
drop off by themselves. The Amandapuss hissed, "JUST JUMP you
idiot!" Certain of certain injury Geni just couldn't bring herself to leap.
"My ankles are not what they used to be; often they crumple beneath
me unexpectedly." This went on for over an hour or so.
Finally, Amy yelled down, "What's happening?"

Other characters in the surrounding environment took notice of
Geni's plight. The white rock had had it. "Just forget it, GET OVER IT!
Go back up, the way that you came, NOW! And get off me—
you're taking up the sun on my back!"
The cellophane grass that grew next to the rock found his comment
very mean. "Can't you leave her alone? Can't you see that she's upset?"
The white rock rebuffed: "Why should I care? There's no other way
of me being me."
The grass responded, "I know you are STUPID, but you simply must
try to learn how to bend."

The multi-colored stripes on the Amandapuss made a flaccid "S" as she
swiveled her torso to lick her shoulder. Geni was on the verge of tears.
She had so wanted to go see the SUN HOUSE ruin, it was the whole
purpose of this trip. She had to do it. She had to. Her anger grew into
exasperation, "If I was a few years younger, I'd risk it. This'll be my only
chance to see it. I CAN'T BELIEVE IT!"

Her black cloud grew out, veiling her eyes when she leaned forward,
making it harder to see. She heard a cat growl. The Amandapuss
whispered, "tough luck, kid, you did everything right, and it's still a
"no go." That comment set Geni off. She marshaled up intense
resentment and defiance and set her feet on the track that ascended
back up to the lip of canyon where Amy was waiting. The Amandapuss
watched. As Geni walked, her feet created small dusty clouds that flew
up in the air.

A cloud above sighed loudly to its neighbor, "Look, look, she's doing
almost what we do."
The cloud beside replied, "Well? So what? We make our impact when
we fall down on the Earth; and then we rise back up again."
The first cloud retorted, "But I want to stay down there all the time."
"Oh, come on, you're always complaining about that. You stay if you
hit a lake, and when you were hail you got to bounce."
The first cloud ticked, "True and maybe we can do that more often—
and if things keep going the way they are going now, we will."
They tittered. The cellophane grass reproached them, "You're so mean,
you're just envious that she can move at will and you can't."

Geni came up out of the canyon and met Amy at the top.
She coughed and used her inhaler; "I'm so angry . . . too steep . . .
I could have DIED . . . If I was two inches taller I could make it . . .
or if I had a rope or someone else to grab onto . . ."
Amy put her arm around her. "You know they told you couldn't use a
rope or ladder. So, it's not your fault."
Geni's transparent black cloud enveloped her body. The backpack wore a
chaotic design, as she repeated angrily, "All that planning, all that money,
my only chance . . ." She inhaled her inhaler.
The Amandapuss snarked, "Better safe than sorry" and disappeared.
Amy, ever steady, coaxed, "Don't put so much pressure on yourself—
just wait, we're still going to have fun."
They headed to the car and drove to meet an archaeological tour group.
They'd camp with them for a few days and see wonderful things.

Archeological Trip

GOING ON an archeological camping trip and being out in Nature would be the best medicine for Geni. It would help fill up that hollow ache embedded inside her: She'd be among other people. They'd hike through desert canyons, where ruins and pictures etched into the rocks from a thousand years ago lived. She was so excited; and Amy was moving pretty well in spite of her foot.

As the group headed to the trailhead the next day, the Native American guide, Henry, met them and announced, "We're not going anywhere today—too muddy. You'd get in there and get exhausted from constantly having to pick up your legs; and then we'd have a lot further to go."
Sam cursed as Geni seethed inside, *I can't believe it. I came all the way out here . . .*
Henry explained, "It usually dries out by now, but we haven't had this much rain during this month before. It never stays this wet, this long."

Amy smelled something and whispered, "Do you smell that? It smells like cat piss . . . but its really strong . . ." Henry sniffed the air. "It's probably a puma, there's one that lives around here."
Joe remarked, "I'd like to see that!"
"Me, too." Henry replied. "I've been out here my whole life, even went looking for them, but never did find one . . ."
Geni had a quiet meltdown with her inhaler.

Back at camp, dinner was tasty. They sat around the fire and toasted marshmallows. They drank beer, played cards, and Joe played guitar.

Venus appeared in the sky. Someone noticed the sequined backpack had grown a picture. "Hey look at that! It looks like a plant stem."
Agnes ran over. "No, it looks like an infinity sign with a line through its center."
Geni educated them, "I love this backpack, it holds all my stuff and it can make its own pictures, like that, all by itself. You can make your own drawings, too." She showed them how to draw in the sequins. They took turns making their own designs.
Geni was grateful they were there. But a few minutes later, she sunk back down inside where her black hole resided:
Today I am with you, My family of sheep,
Someone calls and I follow Blindly.

She wandered over to the edge of the surrounding escarpment to calm herself. She found a plastic mermaid toy and tossed it into her backpack. Unbeknownst to her, the packsack sequins laid out an image of a fish tail.

Ebb and flow. Constant change.
I caught a green germ. Cocooned in its warmth,
Marriage-lit notions of eternity bloomed me into existence.
That city that held promise disappeared a way over there,
a long time ago.
Venus, help me to follow,
to catch and receive, to transmit"

Sleeping would be easy tonight after being outside all day.
Alone in her tent the campfire make flickering changes on the walls.

Don't go back to sleep.
Always the sleepless one, both creator and destroyer
—there's a god that does that, too.
There were always the same things in life.
The saloon keeper
The guitar player
The tossing of cards,
Red shirts and some kind of weapon.
The snowfall has no perfume.
The Kansas fields no end.

Geni started to drift off as it started to rain. Geni and Tom sat waiting for a bus. He pulled out an umbrella and held it over her. It grew larger surrounding her with silhouettes of pine branches shifting behind his face.

An unknown voice rustled:

you look away and try your best not to see me.
I am part of you—the black thorn in your side . . .
the one that won't go away . . . the one who bleeds . . ."

The sounds of ocean waves accompanied this ceaseless phrase that repeated and turned into abstract sound.
A cat roualed. Outside, the wind picked up and tore at a corner of the tent. It opened up a whole side, and everything started to fly out, including her backpack. Geni, being roused awake, threw on her boots. "My inhaler!" She chased the wind that threw sand into her eyes to blind her.

Off and on, she'd catch hold of the shimmering sack. The wind howled. She followed. Everything was in there: her diary, her cell phone, a water bottle, clothing, a flashlight, and THE inhaler. The wind landed her pack next to a cave then pushed it inside, laughing at its trick.

Mummy's Cave

IT WAS pitch dark.
Geni tripped over something and fell, landing beside her pack.
She got out her small flashlight and turned it on.

She had tripped over a mummy.
She freaked out with a little scream and edged away to escape it, shaking.
She caught herself, regrouped, and aimed the light toward it.
She could only see it in small segments.

Slowly, it began to emit a sound and a red glow,
that grew bigger and louder.
She knelt down beside it to examine it closer.
A dense hum that came from a thousand ancestors echoed:

> *You trapped . . .*
> *Where I am,*
> *of being . . .*
> *like I am . . .*
> *attached to you,*
> *I face sure annihilation.*

The glow slowly gathered into the center of the form, and pulsated its light. The voice came from inside it and changed into a command:
There is never and any "real knowing" . . . Take the jewel . . .

Geni stripped away the dirty cloth strips to investigate the red luminescence.

She found the spot, and in that spot a faceted crimson gemstone lay. At first it glistened, like any cut surface, but then it stopped and changed into the dull red color of pipestone. She pocketed it.

Outside, it was starting to clear up. Dawn approached.
Geni stood to leave; hearing again,
You put me outside your walls, but I cling like moss . . .

She stepped out of the cave, and looked back at the corpse.
She was totally lost.

She noticed a fire on a mesa top a way off in the distance and headed that way.

Greed

TWO FIGURES stood by a dwindling camp fire on the mesa's peninsula ledge. They saw Geni approaching.

The younger one, thirty-something, wore binoculars and a long coat. He called out with a British accent; "Hello, did you get caught in the rain? . . . Come up and join us."

"S-H-H-H-h-h-h-h, don't call her" the older man hissed. He had a large, mashed potato body and his clothes were shabby. Geni headed towards them up to the mesa top. The younger one adjusted a telescope and said, "My name is Shackleton. And this is Mr. Smithy."

"Hi, I'm Geni. What are you guys looking at?"

"US!?" the older American lied, "Why, we're anthropologists, scouting about . . ."

"I love anthropology!" Geni remarked. "But I got lost in the storm. I need to get back to my campsite."

Two other men snuck up from the opposite edge of the mesa. They looked to be the same age at Smithy. Unshaved and dressed like ranchers; one looked mean and carried a rifle. Their demeanor suppressed any introductions.

The one in charge spoke, "Why, Smithy, I see you're back . . ."

"Back? What did you expect, Joanus? Smithy challenged.

"This is my spot."

"No, it's not, and you know it," Joanus snorted. He stepped forward and swept his arm from left to right, indicating the ground beneath their feet.

"This is my property."

"Below, perhaps, down there on the plain," replied Smithy firmly, "but, this peninsula is attached to my bank of hills over there; so this peninsula is MY land, and you're standing on, old friend."

They move close together and got in each other's face.

"Boss," replied the one with the gun, "do you want me to . . ."

Geni was a little un-comfortable witnessing this display. She shook her inhaler and debated whether to use it, as it was no longer full.

"Lets not get hasty, gentlemen," the English man countered. "MacFearson, aren't you going to wish the lady "Good Day?" MacFearson grinned a mostly toothless smile and rested his grip on the rifle as he bowed slightly. "Sorry, miss, How are you today? Your hair looks great in this light. I'm . . ."

"Who are YOU?" Joanus bellowed at Geni, while locking eyes with Smithy.

Geni, flustered, tried to reply.

Down below on the plane, a cattle mooed. A few strolled by as some sat or ate grass. "Listen here, Smithy," Joanus pushed, "This land is MINE—it's growing up out of MY FIELD; NOT off of YOUR hill."

Shackleton broke in: "Gentlemen, gentlemen, its another beautiful day, and your cattle look handsome down there on the plane, Mr. Joanus, indeed they do."
He turned toward the one with the rifle and rolled a cigarette.
"Say, MacFearson, how have you been? How's the wife?"

MacFearson looked embarrassed and said, "Well, I haven't seen her, I guess you heard."
"Yes, well, that's too bad . . ."
He handed MacFearson the cigarette and lit it for him.

Geni looked down at the cows and flowers and rocks and tried to decide what to do.

"I say, Joanus, your herd should bring in what this year?" Shackleton carried on in a most friendly manner.
"I'd say a least a hundred thousand, wouldn't you? I think the red and white one is particularly fine, I'd love to have its skin when the time comes. Would you sell that to me? Look how handsome it is . . ."

Joanus's face softened. He broke the stare with Smithy and looked out over the herd, "Where is it?"
"There," Shackleton said pointing with a cigarette, "That one over there—here, use these." He handed Joanus the binoculars. Joanus took them and looked.

"Say, miss," MacFearson moved closer to Geni, "Have you been to Sammy's place in town?"
Geni shook her head "No" and looked at the ground.
"They have steaks and beers from all around the world and you can dance." Geni wanted to leave.

Smithy put his hands in his pockets and touched his gun hidden inside. He raised and lowered himself on his toes. He looked at the telescope. The sun glinted off it. He had to get out of there. He peeked at his sidekick, Shackleton.
Shackleton caught Smithy's glance and turned toward Joanus.
"Yes well, I'd like that REALLY I would. Please don't forget me when the time comes; only a few more months now right? Then you'll have a nice bundle of money, you really will, think of that, think of that . . ."

Joanus got grumbly again. He turned around to face Smithy a few feet away from him.
"Well Smithy, don't you forget what I've said."
"Now, Now, no harm done, no harm done," Shackleton chimed in.
"Ahhh," Joanus fanned his hand at him and moved closer to Smithy.
"This is my parcel and you're not welcome on it, EVER!"
"Well, Joanus, I'm going to call it a night now, it's too bright to see anymore," Smithy replied courteously. He started to pack up the telescope.

Truck Conversation

GENI SAT between Smithy and Shackleton who was driving a pick-up truck down a dirt road. Smithy talked.

"So you see Geni, that's how its been between me and Joanus. He's the kind that needs an enemy. I'm not interfering with anything of his that's important. He's just property nuts, like a lot of other people around here."

His voice became softer, "But they'll gets theirs . . . they'll get theirs . . . and I'll get mine. You know what I'm planning? I'll have more than all of them combined—You see, up there on Neptune, you know the planet, Neptune?"

Geni shook her head "Yes."

"Up there storms form diamonds in the atmosphere. The carbon atoms freeze in the clouds and they start to fall down to the planet's surface because of their weight. But if they hit the surface, it's all over, all over." He looked for her reaction.

"The surface is so hot it changes them back to gas, and then they're destroyed. The trick is to harvest them before they fall back down . . ." He smacked Shackleton with his hand, "That's what Shackleton's designing, a machine that will catch them before they fall back to the surface."

Geni snarled inside, "*I, me, mine.*" She drew the letter "B" into the mermaid sequins: *To "B" or not to "B" . . . what makes the world go round? . . . I consume therefore I am.*

Smithy declared, "We'll be the first ones to get the diamonds and we'll be rich, RICH!" He shook his head and went deeper inside himself. Geni tried to calm herself, "But, what about your piece of land here, isn't that good for something? I mean, its here on EARTH and you're thinking about going to OUTER SPACE??? I don't get it . . ."

Smithy insisted, "Don't you think its a good idea? We'll be so rich I could buy all of your paintings."

Shackleton laughed. Smithy continued, "Wouldn't you want to be just a little bit more comfortable, even just a teeny weeny bit more if you could? How much more paint could you buy?"

The truck pulled over. Geni got out of the cab.

Shackleton indicated, "That's the entrance into the slot canyon. Go through to the end and you'll get back to your people. There's no water until the end, so here's some water, and take this." He handed her some jerky. "Now, you have enough water, and you have something powerful to eat. Full of salt! the elixir of life! Made from the sea and the sun. Better than diamonds!" he cackled.

"Thanks for helping me," she replied.

"It should only take you a few hours to get through," Shackleton asserted. "Take care."

"Goodby, Geni," Smithy said gently. "I hope you find what you're looking for."

That surprised her a little. She waved goodby as they drove off and moved toward the mouth of the canyon.

Probably Toxic

GENI TEXTED AMY: "Got lost, am at the end of the canyon.
Should be there by end of the day, depressed I'm missing out."
A few twenty-somethings exited the canyon; their phones glued
close to their eyes. One guy said, "Service, I LOVE IT."
The girl replied, "I know! My phone is my favorite thing,
I can't stand being without it."

Geni's brain spewed lightning, *People and their stupid cell phones.
Why don't they grasp what's around them.*

She entered into the slot canyon that grew skinny, then wider, then
skinny again. As she wound her way through the twisted channel, the
sun grew higher, and escaped the reach of its walls. At times, it was so
narrow that the walls sandwiched her body. It felt cool.

After about a half mile it opened wider. A tiny pond sported a small
family who were shooting cell phone pictures of themselves.
Geni walked past them along the edge of the water. It would be nice
to cool off. Different colors skimmed the water's surface looking
rather treacherous. The skeleton of a horse laid next to it.

The family yelled happily and removed their clothes to jump in it.
Geni cautioned them forcefully: "Hey don't your think this looks
a little toxic? Look at those colors floating around."

"Its OK," the father said. He was around thirty-five; svelte in tight
clothing, a movie-star type, who knew he was good looking.
The mother in a doughty dress, seemed clueless,
"We come here often."
But what are these colors?" Geni insisted.
"Oh, they're nothing, I love those patterns, I'm an artist."
the man assured her.
Geni wasn't having any of that.
"I'm an artist too, but this looks dangerous, to me."
The man jumped at this news: "Oh, you're an artist?"
"Yeah, but I'm not from around here."
"Hi, I'm Josh and this is Jill, my wife. Where are you from?
do you have a gallery?" He walked over to her.
"No, I'm here on vacation."
"What's your work like?"
The kids tried to engage Geni.
The boy asked, "Miss, miss, do you know if mermaids can drown?
Geni replied to their parents, "You can see my stuff online."
Josh, acted cool. "Do you have anything here I could see?
I'd like to see it in person."
Jill, rolled her eyes; jealous of the attention Josh was paying to Geni.
"Come on, Josh, she just said she's not from around here."
She looked straight at Geni, "Right?"

The kids start to tug at their Mother. "Mom, help us blow up the
inner tube."
Josh cocky, cozied up more. "Have you been out here long?"
Geni recited her tale. He offered to drive her back to the campsite.
Jill had had enough; "It's not that far; you can probably walk it in
a couple of hours."
Josh insisted, "Why don't you join us and then we'll drive you back,
do you have a bathing suit with you?"

The kids chimed in for Geni to come swimming with them.
Geni, tired, contemptuous, cursed to herself. *Why do I always have to be
the one that sees everything?*
She spoke, "You wouldn't get me in there, its not clear and it rained
last night."
Josh off-handedly stated: "I know they dump stuff downriver, but they
said its not harmful."
Jill asked, "Who said that?"
"Jim Jones, you know . . ."
Jill grew rigid, "Listen Josh, he'd say anything—just cause you work for
him doesn't mean he'll tell you the truth."

Images of Tom, Geni's husband, invaded her brain. *Tom, I'm so sorry,
I remember our fights, I so wish you were here now.*

The kids aimed to enter the water.
Geni horrified, tried to yell, "NO" but started to cough and searched
for her inhaler.
Jill scolded the kids.
The kids chorused, "Aw, Mom, why can't we go in?"

Jill turned toward Geni. "My aunts who lived near the waste tanks
downstream got cancer, but the company insisted this area was purified
and de-contaminated."
The kids begged their father. "Dad, Dad, can't we go in?"
Josh said, "Yes, you can."
Jill raised her voice, "No, they can't, and we're leaving, right NOW.
We're going home, Josh, and we're not coming here anymore."
She gathered their stuff together, as the kids whined.

Geni used her inhaler. How obnoxious they are. She resumed her march
calling out, "Nice meeting you," Inside she sneered, *Why can't they see
how awful that was, and just be happy with each other?*

Their voices faded away. The backpack's sequins shaped a water drop.

Geni heard a hum like many voices. *Somehow, it must be coming from
the deceased ancestors circulating throughout the landscape.*

Angel Fight

THE SAND made noise under her steps. The area was exceedingly still. Geni noted many pretty stones, plants and rock formations in the environs, but underneath it all she reflected on that fact that all her family was gone. She was tired of struggling with the waning and waxing of her emotions. Her fear, the depression. She thought seriously about ending it all.

Very slowly, the American Amandapuss became visible and joined her, walking on two legs. Her sneakers were multi-colored. Her striped, mid-thigh length skirt had tulle pieces that stuck out in a funny way. She tried to turn Geni around by egging on her anger:
"It's too bad, that some can't seem to be happy without their 2 houses, SUVs, and side trips to lands of Paradise. Maybe that is happiness for them."

But Geni was too deep in her despair to try to rationalize her pain away.

The Amandapuss tried a different tactic:
"What's the point? Its easier not to care. No more exhaustion, no more disappointments . . ."
Geni asked, *Should I stay or go? This day tricked an exploding bombshell for me.*

The Amandapuss half hissed, half purred, "My abyss holds a lure."

Geni pondered: *If I did end it all, and looked back later, would I be sorry I did it?*

A ringing telephone prompted Geni to cover her ears. The Amandapuss vanished.

A wheelchair bearing her father's frail body was on an iPad screen.
"Dad, Dad, can you hear me?" she voiced loudly.
Two nursing assistants were moving him from assisted living to the hospital; as he had tested positive for COVID 19. There was a tired fear in his eyes.
Geni yelled, trying to make herself heard, while the nurses tried to center his attention on her.
"What? what? I can't hear you," he mumbled.
At least he still knew her.
The nurses translated what she said to him but he didn't seem to register the situation as she said, "Goodbye."

Geni started to cry. She knew there was nothing she could have done. She felt helpless. She gathered herself together and walked, stopping every now and then to use her inhaler.

She kept moving forward. Shadows shifted across one side of the canyon to the other; changing from green to red. As time passed the rocks started to seem threatening rather than neutral.

Geni took stock of herself: *My Generation was born out of the generation who went to the war, after the GREAT WAR, to end all wars. Our parents were all soldiers. Some faced death, some held the home front, after that there were other struggles: equal rights, South East Asia, and more wars back in Europe over ideologies and migrations. 9/11, COVID, and more struggles brought forth . . . Thinking about it, I don't believe they'd want me to give up no matter what I'm feeling.*

She felt her black cloud stir. It seems to have hidden itself inside her backpack.

A man, fifty-ish, dressed in chinos, hiking boots and a denim shirt came up quickly behind Geni.
"Excuse me, Ma'am, but there's something sticking out of your backpack, it looks like its going to fall out."
Geni stopped.
He grabbed her dark, transparent cloud and yanked,
"I can take care of that for you . . ."
Geni fumbled, "What are you doing!?"
He kept pulling; unraveling the cloud as if it was fabric, and wound it around his hand asking, "Who are your ancestors?"
Geni became angry, and turned toward him, "Who are you?"

"Who are you?" the man mimicked. "I'm the angel, Gene Gibbons, here to help you. You don't need this."

With most of the cloud wrapped around his hand, he stepped backwards, to abscond with it.
"STOP THAT!" she yelled, hearing the voices of a thousand dead fade in.
"What would you care, if it just disappeared?" he taunted.
Geni defended herself: "It's mine, why would you want it anyway?"

They played tug of war, and scuffled.
"Give it back!"
"You don't want it."
"Leave me alone!"
"It's of no use to you."

She gave him a big push. He fell down and laughed. The cloud sprawled out on the ground. It had acquired a shimmering pattern.
Geni grabbed some dirt and threw it in his face. "GO AWAY! and don't come back."

She heard a sound above her on the top of a ledge.

She saw the black tip of a puma's tail dart away. When she looked back a second later, the man was gone. Footprints in the dirt showed where they had fought.

Geni seized her precious accessory, shoved it into her backpack, and tramped quickly up the narrow canyon.

Hydra Parade

THE LIGHT in the blue was recasting itself as twilight.

I wonder how long this is going to take. I wonder if they're looking for me. Maybe I went the wrong way. Geni would have to sleep there. She started to gather some wood. The air took on a smell of baking bread. There was a sound of crashing ocean waves.

Above her on an overhang, Geni caught sight of a female. They stared at each other. She was a mermaid. She uttered, "You were right," and dove off the stone shelf and landed in the middle of the sandy ground between the slot canyon's walls. It swallowed her as if it were liquid.

Geni gasped. She walked around the spot testing it with her foot, and sat down to drink some water.
"Are you going to come back?" she asked loudly.
She lingered: relaxed, waiting, anticipating.

A small movement materialized out of a crack between the rock face and the ground that met it. It swished and grew larger. It was a hydra, moving slowly and awkwardly the way that they do. The creature stretched and flipped, struggling to move toward the center where the mermaid vanished. Other hydras arose, and stumbled, following the first. Geni jumped from one side to the opposite trying to get a better view; but settled onto her stomach to watch.

A locust-like hum grew loud and steady. The mermaid's voice ascended up from the earth.

"THE HYDRA is an invertebrate that regenerates its body with fresh cells. Hydras don't show any signs of deteriorating with age. HYDRAS can divide and differentiated any cell from their body. In humans, these kind of cells are present only at the start of embryonic development. The hydra can constantly renew its body. They may, in fact, be immortal."

The first hydra made it to the place where the mermaid went and plunged down below the surface of the ground. This leisurely parade continued as dusk, then darkness overtook the sky. Sounds of the sea escorted the hydras. As more and more of them dropped below the floor it turned marshy with water that seeped upwards. The full moon appeared and its reflection settled onto the lake-y wetness.

When the last hydra dove in, Geni took the red jewel rock out of her pocket and placed it on the Moon's reflection. As the water absorbed back into the earth, she thought, *So, the key must be, NOT to get rid of the past, but discover a way to engage with it.*

Geni pulled the rock back into her pocket, and made a fire. She tried to text Amy, but there was no service.

Inside a dark grotto close by, the eyes of a feline glowed.

Yes, I know you are near. That would be something, to be killed by a big cat. But this is the perfect place to arrive at the big sleep—to go out and never come back. I'm so peaceful after observing that procession.
She leaned against a large stone and slept.

Mother Earth

THE DAWN brought a loud blast in the distance, followed by a puma ROAR. Geni tried to text again, but it was a no go. An old fragile, woman in a white antique lace dress came down the channel calling, "Buddy, are you there, Buddy?" This scared Geni.

"Hello, did you see my son down there? A little boy?" Geni shook her head "No." She knew this woman as her grandmother. The woman in a white, still continued to call, "Are you there? Where are you? . . . Buddy?" and moved down the canyon's trail.

Geni was a bit shaken by this encounter. She got up and touched the spot where the creatures had disappeared the night before, drank some water, and began walking her course. The shadows moved from one side of the canyon to the other; changing from green to red like a Giorgione painting, then back again.

A few pebbles fell from above. Geni looked up. It was her mother who had died at eighty-five; dead now for nine years. Except now she looked like she was forty. A Spanish fandango on a harpsichord snuck in from somewhere.

"Mom! What are you doing here?" "There! Do you hear that?" her mother asked. She loved classical music. She played it all day long, everyday. Her mother scrambled down the rocky ledges. "Mom, did you do that?" Geni cried out. Her mother smiled, "I came to join you on a little walk." Now Geni looked like she was ten years old. "How's your trip going?" They proceeded down the passage.

Geni proffered, "Mom, I've been thinking about things, recently. I must have been a thorn in your side." "No," Mom replied; but Geni interrupted her. "I was always at odds with things. I tried to solve everyone's problems, everywhere, all the time. She started to cry and looked for a tissue in her backpack, but all she found was a yellow leaf that she tossed aside. Geni continued, "It's taken up too much of my time."

Her mother now looked as if she was twenty years old. She touched Geni's shoulder, and sighed, "You just have to find a new way, a new attitude." She leaned into Geni, "Sometimes, the coldness of death brings clarity."

The canyon turned and opened up on one side onto a green field.
The woman in white lay sick in a bed.
Geni's mother cried, "Ah, there's Mama. Poor Mama."
Geni's two aunts stood ten feet away from her. One wore a lavender, high necked, fine ribbed wool sweater dress. The other aunt was in oversized flannel pajamas that had fat, vertical, royal blue and white stripes on it. She was a little bent over with osteoporosis.
Geni's Mon turned toward her and said, "That's where I inherited it, you know, and then later, you were imprinted."

They passed them by.
"History is in your soul. We were together for a long time. Now it's your turn at life."

Geni felt like she was twenty.
My life could have been so different. But, if I took what I wanted, there wouldn't be enough left for you, Mom. And then you'd leave me.

"Mom," Geni sniffed out loud, "I tried to help you"
Her mother seemed to be sixty. "Oh, don't be silly, I gave you help."
Geni wasn't sure about that: it didn't feel that way to her.

"Mom, Why did you come here?"
Her mother replied, "Have you heard the legend? The Great Spirit told the children that they were made from pipestone."
Geni realized with surprise, "Mummy?"

Her mother continued, "The ground where it was found was to be sacred."
Geni got a hold of herself; she'd wrestle with that information later.
"Mom, I'm lonely without you, in spite of how I judge our relationship."
Mother continued: "No weapons must be used or brought upon it."

Her mother started to become transparent.
Geni panicked, "WAIT! WAIT!"
Now that her Mother was fading, it was impossible to tell her age.
Geni yelled, "Mom, you didn't tell me anything, Mom! . . . MOM!"
"You will see, you will find a way to use it over and over in time."

Her Mother faded away completely: "You're safe, I'll be right here."
Geni sighed, "I'm so tired. Its too hard to be happy: it would be so much easier to just join you."

The sequins set themselves in a spiral pattern.

Radio

GENI HEARD static coming from around the bend. She headed down the channel again. Eventually, one side opened out. A broad view of low dirt mounds studded with rocks had an escarpment behind them. Was this the end of the canyon?

Two middle-aged males fooled with a radio box almost a century old. Their hats shaded their faces as they tried to tune it in. They held sandwiches wrapped in wax paper and took turns, eating and fumbling.

A little boy dressed in shorts and cowboy boots ran up to Geni. "Hey, What's your name? I'm Joey. Do you want to have lunch with us?" He pushed an unwrapped sandwich toward her. Geni smiled, "thanks, I'd love that." They moved thirty feet away from the men, and sat on some short rocks.

The boy was about five years old. He continued to chatter, asking many things. He offered her a carton of juice. His own carton sat open on a rock beside him. A hummingbird buzzed by.
Geni remarked, "I bet that bird can smell your juice."
He looked disinterested and became quiet. He asserted a more focused notion. "Do you know what I wanna be when I grow up?—a wizard. They can do anything, they can go through doors and change things into something else, and . . ."

One of the men perked up. He walked straight over and looked directly into Joey's eyes.

"Joey, we've talked about this before. There are no such things as wizards."
Joey, shocked, knocked over his juice. Geni angered at the man's reprimand: *Another moron.*

The man walked back to his work. The other man said, "Look. The crystal's cracked . . . it worked the other day."

Geni looked at Joey. He had dropped the last bit of his sandwich on the dirt. The neighborhood ants gathered together for a feast.
Geni knelt down in front of him. "You know, I have a secret . . . I believe in wizards and their power. You never know when you might meet one, it may take many, many years . . ."
Their eyes met. Joey leaped towards her and they hugged.
"But," she resumed, "its kind of a secret, you know what I mean? Not everyone gets it; and you don't have to tell them about it."
He nodded.

Geni picked up a stick. "Do you like to draw? " She drew a circle around him; "LOOK! There you are in the middle of your empire!"
Joey threw his arms out wide, "My empire!"
"And no one can bother you or disturb you in any way when you are inside it. It's like your castle." MY CASTLE!" Joey exclaimed.
Geni drew a wavy shape. "Look I made a spiral . . ."
"Awesome," he affirmed. She handed him a stick. "I'm going to make a snake," he uttered and started to draw.

After a while, Geni made her way over to the two men crouched
over the radio.
"Thanks for lunch, what are your guys doing?"
The second one looked up and said, "We've been trying to get
this working, our friend is supposed to contact us. I think the
crystal cracked."

Geni deflated her feelings toward the first man,
"I may have something that will help."
She reached for her red rock that appeared in crystal shape.
"Here, try this."
The men strapped it in place. It started to pick up the Fandango
harpsichord music she had heard earlier. They smiled.
"Lets try to contact Jim, maybe he'll still be there."

They turned the dial and picked up a news report:

"GOOD DAY! It is February 2, 2020 and this is Steve Good."
Static blotched through the commentator's report:
"Dynamiting is taking place in the National Cactus Park for the
Southern border wall. (static crackled) The TRUMPET administration
has circumvented the Aboriginal Protection Act propelling their action
ahead." (static crackled)
Rep. Johnson tweeted Monday that the hill with warriors' graves has
been defiled with construction equipment . . . (static) . . . nationally . . .

(static) . . . and ancient Saguaro have been crushed . . . (static) . . .
a natural spring has been dammed . . .
The . . . (static) . . . did not res . . . (static) . . . for comment.
"Their complete disregard of . . . (static) . . . Johnson said (static) . . .
borders Mexico . . .
The sound crackled and faded away.

The first man joked, "A ha! more disturbances!"
The second added, "Well, you know he don't have no DAY of the
DEAD in his life."
The first replied, "That's the problem!"
The second laughed: "I hear Hitler said that when he died, he wouldn't
even need a grave marker, 'cause everyone would know where to find
him—he was so well-liked." They laughed and handed the rock back to
her. "Thank you, Mommy, that worked great!"

Geni threw the rock into her backpack and heard glass breaking.
It was her cellphone. *Oh well, I'll get over it.*
She spoke jauntily as she headed out, "Hey guys, which is the way back
to the campground?"
One pointed, "Right around that rock, down that trail."
"Goodbye and good luck with that radio . . ."
They tipped their hats, "Thanks, Mommy, you be careful out there."
As she ambled away, she heard, "I bet he can't name his relatives back
six generations like I can . . ."

Goblin Valley's Camel

AROUND THE BEND, through a short passage, and a little ways after, the vista opened out onto a vast landscape with no end. It was populated with oddly shaped pillars and shapes of compressed earth. Many looked like giant mushrooms or oversized goblins. Some looked like animals laying in rest.

How aesthetic.

Physically hot, with all her water gone, Geni decided, This is it.

I don't have to care anymore, I've seen my share and I can just go to sleep, and that will be that. It won't be so bad to die that way.

Geni laid down against a rock's shadowed side, and started to doze off, but felt thorns pricking her. She opened her eyes.

A butterfly was licking the sweat off her arm. Its feet felt like claws.

Suddenly, the mud-rock's head took on a camel face that started to talk, "Hello there. Aren't you thirsty?"

Geni very surprised, responded, "Um . . . yeah, but . . ."

The camel said, "I know where there's a watering hole sixty feet away."

Geni replied emphatically, "Oh, no. No. I'm Ok. Please, go on without me."

"What? Me travel alone?" the animal-rock replied.

Geni got annoyed, "Well why not? I was alone."

The Camel, an international flaming creature, whispered,

"The water there is crystal clear, and so delicious." They paused.

The Camel said, "Did you know sometimes our mothers reject us and refuse to suckle us? But they come round after they hear a certain kind of music. They cry tears. And then they resume feeding us."

"I know," replied Geni, nicely, but un-impressed. "I saw a film about that. How did you come to be here?"

"We have eternal patience. We are always here," the camel replied.

"We've adapted to our environment, but yet, we can still die and do."

"I've never ridden on a camel," said Geni.

The Camel sighed, "I guess that's what people think of us. Just modes of transportation."

Geni, surprised, looked away embarrassed, "I'm sorry. I'm sure you have your own life that's important to you."

"Yes," it softly hissed, naturally (this was not a hiss of distain).

"Water does seems to be scarce around here." Geni noted politely.

"You ARE really rude! No doubt that's your way of addressing the condition of my hump," the Camel admonished her. "Did you know that we can shift the water around inside our humps?"

"No, I didn't know that," Geni responded.

"Yes, we create our own unique designs using the water inside our humps to shape our flesh." Geni was fascinated in this phenomena.

"Mine IS in a sorry state right now because of the drought."

"Really?!" Geni paused and looked inquisitive.

"Oh yes," the camel now feeling encouraged, continued,
"We push a little water over here, and some over there; it's like
landscaping, except it's fur, you see, instead of grass. Most people don't
notice, but we do. In fact, that's our pride and joy, our status among
each other. If only we had some water nearby, I could demonstrate,"
she sighed.

Geni looked straight into the face she saw.
"I hope I didn't make you feel bad, before."
She reached out to touch her but it seemed silly, as this was only dirt.
She pulled her hands back and put them behind her.
She picked up her face and looked pleasantly at the camel:
Please tell me more."

The Camel stirred and a new bit of energy filled her eyes.
"Well, you see, it doesn't last forever, not like a painting or a
famous book. But it's what we can do," she said nodding her head
enthusiastically.
"It describes something of us, while still being curtailed by our own
particular limitations . . ."

"And when we are finished with our creation, we stand in a chosen
spot, against some backdrop that compliments our creation—
that's part of it, too. It has to do with sensing the environment.
Everyone has to talk about it and show off, or it doesn't count at all.
It's a structure, belonging to our group . . . You understand, don't you?"

"Oh Yes," said Geni enthusiastically. "So can you show me? If you get
some water? I think I'd like to see that."

Geni started to dust herself off.

The camel replied, "Of course."
They proceeded off in the direction toward the spring.
"I went to see Thrinta's showing last year" the Camel continued,
"Oh, by the way we haven't introduced ourselves. "I'm Ella."
"And I'm Geni," Geni replied.

"Yes, as I was saying, Thrinta was usually all the rage. Everyone was a
little envious of her work, but this last piece,"
Ella gave out big exhaled air that had its own distinct sound.
"She had these ripples running through her form and could shift them
over to a different location. It didn't work at all . . ."

Geni remained quiet.
"Oh yes, you should have see it, it was ridiculous! First of all, it would
make your eyes start to cross, which can be painful to us."
Ella tilted her head down into Geni's face. "Yes, at one time Thrinta was
on top, but not anymore."
Geni nodded, "Really, I'm glad you're telling me this, and its very
interesting, but I can't really imagine."
"But, you do catch my drift, don't you?" said Ella rolling her eyes.
Geni shrugged, "I guess so."

"If only I could get enough water, you'd see what I can do and that
would explain it."
"I want to see it!," Geni conjoined.
Ella clucked lowly, then said emphatically. "I LIKE you, you don't seem
to be a person at all." (She caught herself abruptly at her remark.)
"Thanks for the compliment," Geni replied.

They reached the spring. Geni saw the mermaid's face hovering over it.
The Camel urged, "Have some."
"No, no, I'm not thirsty. But I do want to see what you come up with."
Geni looked around to avoid Ella's eyes.

The Camel sighed crossly, "I showed you where it is,
and it's VERY DIFFICULT for me to MOVE."
Geni shook her head. "No, I don't need any water."
Ella chided her, "Oh, Who cares if you die?"
"Exactly," Geni said. An uncomfortable pause occurred.

The Camel got huffy, calmed down, and assumed a reverie,
"Do you remember Pedigree pencils?"
Geni was surprised that the camel knew that.
"They were a turquoise color, with black at the bottom?
Well, once I twisted some of MY fur—the curly section on the right,
so that it could capture that color blue. You'd have to do it no sooner
that 5 p.m. in October, because it reflected the sky color, obviously.
It wouldn't last past 6 p.m., but it was really beautiful.

I could hardly see it myself, because my neck twists only so far."
Geni nodded: "Ella, how do you know about Pedigree Pencils?"

"Lucille Ball taught me; she sits right here in this spot. She was
a beautiful woman, most people don't think that because she was a
comedian, but she was. Oh, don't looked so surprised, we know all the
movie stars. And over here, on my right shoulder sits Ava Gardner and
my left hip is Joan Crawford, like when she did that."
Ella thrust her hip out; like in a dance number. Geni was perplexed.
Ella looked like an "X." Her neck stretched out over her right shoulder,
as her right leg extended and twisted over towards her other side.
Geni mused, *What different lives we all have.*

Ella stated matter-of-factly: "Oh, we know everything about your
humans. Yes, we have to, because you own us and can move us around
at will . . . sell us off, you know. We have NO say in that. It must have
been a glorious time when we roamed the deserts free. We could find
the watering holes, instead of being tied up and staked the wrong
way in the wind. Some humans are so stupid! You KNOW what
I mean!"

Geni giggled, "Simpatico!" She coughed and gave in. She scooped up
some water in her hand and drank it.
Ella had accomplished her secret goal, but kept that to herself.
"I'm so happy just to adorn myself in some way that makes me feel
beautiful—not like some old piece of dirt. You DO know what I mean?"

"Yes, its your art form," Geni responded, but thought, *You haven't become jaded to it, like I have.*
The Camel said, "Yes, we share that . . ." They both drank some more water.
Ella insisted, "It's absolutely paramount to channel negativity into some form of creativity; don't you think? Imagination sets us apart. You focus on something else, its fun, and it works! That's what art is all about. Don't you agree?"

Geni just filled up her canteen and ignored her.
Ella poked her. "I see I can talk to you! You're like the ocean, moving in every direction, full of different colors. What color would you be, if you could be a color?"
"Humm, changes every day," Geni replied, "but I do like purple a lot."
"Yes, like the mountains," Ella said excitedly. "It stays, that's a good color. Red is nice, too; it has energy, but it can also be jealous . . ."
Then Ella broached, 'So, why are you here? What are you about?"
Geni said, "Well, basically, I've had it. My family is gone, so I came here to get away and see something beautiful and magical. And then I got lost, and now I'm missing out on my trip, and I'm so angry!"
Geni felt heavy as lead. She started to tear up.

Ella stated matter-of-factly, "Oh! I'm sorry, but you know, you really don't need them . . . I mean, what are you gonna do? It's all just life."
Geni's inhaler was out of juice. "I don't know what to do . . ."
Ella hissed, "I talked to my sister in Cincinnati, the other day, her child is nothing but problems, but listen, you don't need anybody, I mean, look at me."

But this attitude didn't resonate with Geni. She unfolded into collapse and had to sit down.
Ella coaxed, "Look to your art . . . look to the EARTH: it will guide you."
Geni noticed Ella was starting to fade away.
"OH, NO! Don't leave now!" Geni agonized.
Ella started to shriek, "It IS getting harder for me to move, now. All this dust seems to be weighing me down!"
Geni begged, "Please, please don't go!"
"I don't understand it at all; but I'm OK, I'm still up and breaking even!"
Ella chirred, "Lots of luck, and remember what I said, and thanks for your thoughtful camaraderie,"
Then she was gone; only the dirt shaping her remains remained.
Geni cried, but got up, and moved on, it was starting to get dark.

Amanda Puma

GENI'S THOUGHTS talked back to her: *must force a new turn of events . . . make a NEW life . . . now . . . a new experience . . .*
The Amandapuss slipped in and rowled cat-ily:
"Is that the question, the question to get to, what's the question? Who gets to ask it? Flip and flop, across and through."
Geni bounced into conversation: *Not now, too tired.*
This was not the time for a debate. She invited an urge of forgetfulness to take over, forever.
The Amandapuss prattled on, "Bad habits fold when the mirror drops."
My problems are still the same. I AM a widow now . . .
The Amandapuss countered, "Desire, want, longing—what do we put on the other?"
Can't you see: They haunt me: Tom, Mom, Dad . . . I will never see them again . . .
The Amandapuss interrupted, "A hole full of water can drown a puddled heart."
Water, sweat, the blood in the sand, what's the difference?
The Amandapuss cantillated, "Water expands once inside the atmosphere. In the beginning there was liquid: TEARS. Too much liquid turns to ice. Deadly. Evermore . . ."
Geni was floored. *What?!*
The Amandapuss patiently stated, "You are not the water, You are not the torrent, You are not the puddle."

A magnetic force yoked them together into a swaying dance-like movement.

Please, Geni wondered, *Can you tell me, will my longing and aloneness ever stop?*
The felined creature explained, "Let go. Say "goodbye.""
N-o-o-o-o-o-o, I can't.
"Visualize a new story . . ."
No. No new story.
"Try and imagine"
too tired to imagine.
"What!? . . . No imagination? . . . No new invention?"
I'm too exhausted to think. Please just let me alone.

With that, a puma faded in and circled around them. It too, could talk:
"Now then . . . Then and now . . . Now and then . . . Who IS the Mother of invention?"

The Amandapuss started singing in a sing-song way,
"Mother, oh mother, where art thou?"
The Puma pertly pattered, "WHO is the Mother of INVENTION?"
Geni replied: *I'm too old to be a mother . . .*
The Amandapuss rebuked her, "oh mother, is that the question?"

Geni's solution surfaced:
I guess I really should chose whether to stay or go.
"Is that the question? . . . the question to ask?" the cats resounded,
"Who are you?"
I wish I knew, Geni conceded.
The three of them erupted across the desert in a fast swirl heading
for who knows where.

The Amandapuss used different tones while continuing to duplicate
her question, "Mother, oh mother, where art thou? Mother, oh mother,
     where art thou? Mother, oh mother . . ."
Geni yelled, "QUIET! I could be happy just to die here!"
     "Mother, oh mother, where art thou? Mother, oh mother,
     where art thou? Mother, oh . . ."
Geni roared, "COME ON! I'm tired of hanging on with my claws.
They're not as strong as yours!"
     "Mother, oh mother, where art thou? . . . Mother, oh mother . . ."
     The puma taunted her, "Mom & Dad . . . Jill & Josh . . ."
Geni roared: "WOULD YOU STOP THAT!? NOW!"
She tried to break free of them, but the Puma continued to
ridicule her:
     "Smithy and MacFearson; people & their stupid cell phones . . ."

Geni shrieked, "All I wanted was to come out here, to see something
beautiful, to re-balance myself."
The cats trilled in chorus, "See me? . . . Purr-c . . . eive me."
Geni screeched: "But I was THWARTED from all that!"
     "See me? . . . Purr-c . . . eive me."
"That stupid rock—WHY couldn't I jump?"
Geni cried out, "If only I could see . . . If only I could see the truth."

The wind struck faster and acrobated around them, making the three
dance more crazily.

Geni anguished inside, *Is there something, something bigger out there?*
     "See me? . . . Purr-c . . . eive me."
Is there something I'm not seeing?
     "See me? . . . Purr-c . . . eive me."
Or is this just it? Geni had reached her crescendo.
Desperately she asked, *If only I knew, if only I knew.*

Raindrops started to fall from the sky.

The Puma and Amandapuss disappeared from sight and sound.

Porcupine

THE RAIN jarred Geni. She had to find shelter—the ground became too slippery to walk upon. She spotted a mud cluster with a womb-like space carved out of it. She crawled in and huddled. Her head almost touched the ceiling. If she sat with her legs crossed in meditation style it was tough, but easier. Her backpack twinkled on her lap. She felt the warmth the compacted mud had drawn from the sun that day. The rain made a curtain of sound and cast a bright fabric of dripping drops of light over the opening, which she could not see beyond.

It had grown dark and lightning flared occasionally. She heard a rustle. Two tiny eyes glowed at the entrance. It moved away, but came back again. The weather was unforgiving. Geni sat still but hummed a little bit, so it would know she wasn't part of the lumpen mud. It stopped. She smelled its odor. A lightning strike revealed them both to each other.

The fat meatloaf with multi-striped spikes was a greenish-tan porcupine. Geni was into sharing but knew if it felt threatened it could attack using its stinky pronged prick-a-presses hidden on its lower back. It whimpered its way into the non-existence space. Geni sat very still. She spoke to the animal mentally, *I know you probably can't see me but I'm here and won't hurt you.*

It looked up at her face. Geni put her hands on top of her head like a prisoner of war. It climbed onto her lap and nested inside her back pack. It was kind of cute, in a funny way.
"What's your name, little one?"
"Rosette," it replied.

The rain kept on pouring down. Rosette's appearance galvanized Geni into a different direction. There was no way she could move until the animal moved out first. Geni sang a lullaby in her head and the animal seemed to get more comfortable. They loosened up and united into a linkage that had an uplifted air like Scarlatti's piano works.

Geni caught the animal's story thru fleeting impressions. Rosette was up in a tree, a typical place for a porcupine, when a forest fire swept thru. The tree caught fire. She had to jump away from it. Rosette answered her impending questions: "Yes, I needed to get down, but it was too high. If I had jumped I would have died. What should I do? I looked around: Fire, Wood: those elements delineate number 50 in the Book of Changes. That meant I had to wait for the right moment or I couldn't survive the fall, you see."
Somehow, this sounds familiar . . . I'm going to put down my arms, now, Geni warned.

Rosette communicated further, "And so, I waited. Eventually, the tree collapsed down to a certain height, and then I let go."

Geni thought, *I'm VERY sorry that happened to you.*

Rosette responded, "People are careless with the environment, hence, many forest fires."

Geni raged out loud, "That's one reason why I'm ready to go. People are so hateful! They're unconscious and uncaring. They're devoid of love. They're . . ."

Rosette interrupted, "Love can't be completely exorcized from any vision. It underlies everything. Love can be hard to see . . ."

"Love?!" Geni chided.

"Conflicting emotions may be caused by unresolved grief. I have acknowledged my issues and forgiven others—that is the real key."

Geni said, "But, how CAN you forgive?"

"Quelling the ego helps," Rosette replied gently.

Geni responded in a softer way, "Maybe if I could see why, why they did what they did, I could at least tolerate them."

Rosette replied, "SEEING may register what's unbelievable to us."

Geni was incredulous, "But, don't you get it? Seeing them is what drives me mad. Why don't they . . ."

Rosette suggested, "Sensitivity can become what sustains you; to deal with the problems of life: to connect to love."

"Life!" Geni finally responded, ". . . I almost forgot about that . . ."

Rosette prodded her, "Look at 'the now' and see the elements surrounding you to discover what your problem means. There is no future, you know."

"Well, it CERTAINLY seems that way for me!"

"Not funny," Rosette firmly replied, "See, examine, and then transform."

"BUT, I want . . ."

"Desire can pull us around.. Desire is the ego's eye."

The animal started to rummage thru the backpack.

"Oh! Look at this!" she said, as she tossed out Geni's inhaler.

"Hey, I need that!" Geni protested, startled.

Rosette picked up the inhaler and held it up over her head.

It had changed into a metal Ding. "Allow your ego to die to see—see?"

Geni was amazed. "What is that? "

Rosette answered, "A Ding. The vessel for an offering to the ancestors. Cultivate your vessel, and you will see."

Geni didn't get it. "Offering?"

Rosette clarified, "Yes, cook up something to offer, toss it into the field of love, and wait to see what happens."

Geni countered, "But what about all my problems?"

"Change is key! . . . If you want change, you must change."

"But how can I change without my ego getting in the way?"

"Examine deeply. You could try asking the Book of Changes; its a great asking tool. Ask it for help to make changes. Stay present."

Geni grew quiet, contemplating that message. "I guess it is all about
desire, the desire to pursue, to achieve a certain result. But how
do you see more deeply, without letting desire and the ego get
in the way?"
Rosette answered "Learn to read the signs."
Geni grew curious, "What do you mean?"
Rosette explained, "I needed to find answers to my troubles.
Unless I took action to get to the root of things, there was no
possibility of evolving. I found working with the Book of Changes
to be helpful."

Geni parried, "I get it, you STUDIED some book . . ."
The porcupine answered, "I DO it by asking for answers,
and discover stimulating dialogue regarding my predicaments.
I enter the Uniting Field."
Geni, now intrigued, pressed on, "Where is that Field?"
"It underlies everything; in physics it's electromagnetism."
Geni quipped, "OK, now I don't get it."
Rosette explained, "Its physics. We can see matter: your backpack,
this dirt. All matter is composed of quantum energy, which appears as
particles and behaves as rippling waves, that form our universe."

"So, you're saying that we are not separate from the field, that we are
also a part of the field."
Rosette confirmed, "Right. And when performing any kind of divination,
you engage with the field to get a reply to your question."
Geni responded, "OK, OK, So, there's no subject and no object,
THERE'S JUST ONE VIEW!"
"Well, there's just one view at that time you're specifically looking
for it."
"And that's the time you get the answer to the question."
"Yes," Rosette clarified, "but remember, energy is always changing.
Your answer catches at the particular time you engage with it."

Geni was confused, but captivated.

She grew quiet and composed herself:
Adapting to change . . .
She announced, "Acceptance of what happens,
adapting to change. That has to become my bottom line."
Rosette snoozily mumbled, "Yes. Anyway, lets get some shut eye,
I'm tired. Tomorrow I have to find a new place to live . . ."

Another Dream

THERE WAS a sound. A low, dull, thud of being underwater. Geni was swimming in a huge sea with hundreds of other people.

That changed. She was back in her apartment; holding the one-inch, antique paper salt container, labeled PERSONAL SALT, that lived in the china closet. It fell down on the wooden floor. A trickle of water crept across the boards next to her bare feet.

Her aunt was there. Her glasses reflected flashes of light. She gestured wildly yelling a warning, but no sound of her voice was heard.

She grabbed Geni's hand and pulled her toward her while walking backwards. Her other aunt stood a few feet away, dressed in the same flannel pajamas with over-sized royal blue and white vertical stripes that she wore in the field next to Grandmother's bed. Geni felt something wet through her boot and woke up.

As the rain continued outside, the water had started to pool inside their nesting spot.

Geni shouted, "Quick, Rosette! We have to get out of here!"

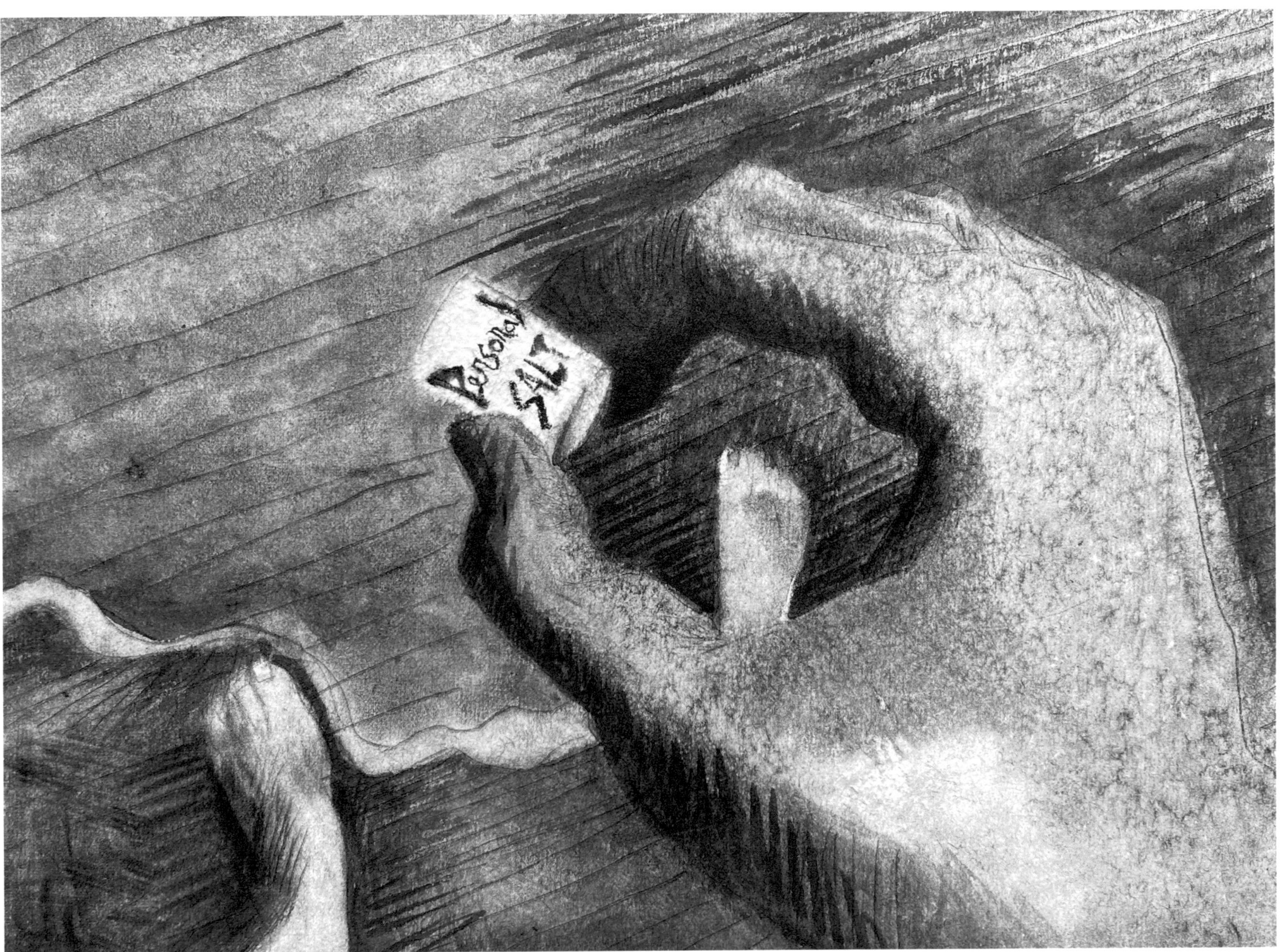

Personal
SALT

Escaping to Return

TUMBLING OUT of their cave, booming sounds shook the Earth. Water ran over the ground and surrounded the higher outcroppings of dirt and rocks. It grew higher and stronger. The voices of one thousand ancestors sung in chorus.
Geni carried the porcupine inside her backpack.
She climbed the ledges towards the top of the mesa to escape the rising flood. A petroglyph on the rock had a line with a spiral on each end.
Geni's black cloud poured out and spread around her body, growing into a web-like net.

As the rain, the thunder, the lightning stormed, a giant, rippling grid rolled and moved water-like in one immense blanketed surface.
They were trapped there.
Geni was knocked off her feet. She started to flop like a fish.
Corpuscles down deep inside her filled with pressure. She howled in pain.

The voices grew louder, embellishing the landscape. Spangly spots appeared in the UNITING FIELD and changed into faces that dotted its vast, deep, shifting perspective.

Geni's body started to sway and twist like a hydra changing positions: first vertical, then horizontal, over and over again. She flowed with the flow of the surroundings.

She grew a mermaid's tail and screamed as the field expanded into greater complexity.
As she swam, the pressure inside her let up and every cell felt like it was full of exploding light. The water continued to rise. Wings appear out of her back as she changed into a bird.
I know I am, but I don't know what I am.

She flew off towards the mesa top, hovered over its surface, and yelled, "Jump! Jump out, Rosette!"
The porcupine sprang out and landed on the ground.
Suddenly everything stopped.

The porcupine, shaken and alone, was safe.
Geni had disappeared from view. Rosette called and called for her extending one hand toward the heavens.

A short time later she saw Geni walking towards her.
She had changed again, into full grown puma.
Rosette tried to decide if she should assume a posture of defense.
She hunkered down and make herself into a small mound.
Geni approached her, sniffed her head, and licked her.

"You ok?" she asked.

The Floodplain

GENI TIRED and pensive, wore her backpack in front of her, and stroked Rosette inside. She walked through a floodplain where uprooted broken tree trucks littered the ground. Birds flew out of the shrubbery and swept by narrowly missing them. In spite of last night's adventure, Geni still sensed a blackness. Her cloudy dark feeling now dragged behind her like a bride's train. Peacock blue faces of a million ancestors sparkled in a crackly field.

That was the greatest experience of my life. But will my blackness ever go? The sound of a thousand ancestors' voices faded up.
Rosette said, "We have walked the ground of the ancients. Can't you sense your ancestors around you? Forgetting them not honors them."
Geni replied, "I guess I can't see very well, yet, but the cries of the birds pierce my heart."

I can mourn. I am not my emotions. I can choose. Choose to be happy.

Geni stopped and set down the backpack to let the animal out.
I guess there's only two things: love and power. Love is the glue that holds the world together.
Rosette remarked, gently, "You have begun your new phase."

I have a new chance. There's only so much time left.

Ahead, a vast landscape lay wide open in deep perspective.

Geni's black train sucked up underneath her shoulder blades and disappeared. They heard a puma purr.

Geni picked up a quill from the ground, tears welling in her eyes, "Rosette, you don't know how much I'll miss you. Many from my world are dead, but I'm alive, on my own pathway."
Rosette replied, "We had a grand time, and there's certainly a lot of food around here to eat. It looks like I can move right in."

Geni saw a strange looking plant, "What is that?"
"It's buckwheat, but not the kind that you can eat."
They laughed at their little joke.
"Rosette, I love you, and I've learned so much. I will never, ever forget it! THANK YOU!"
"It was nothing." Rosette replied. "Be well!" and she waddled off.

The eyes of the Amandapuss slowly appeared in the sky.
This world is amazing.
Geni remembered the petroglyph she had seen. She dragged her finger through the backpack's sequins. When she looked up, the eyes of the Amandapuss had changed into puma eyes.
This world is extraordinary.
The porcupine, walking down the road, caught her thought and answered, "Yes! Yes, it is, and sparks of joy light it up."

Back at Camp

GENI ARRIVED at her campsite an hour later. The hikers
surrounded her. Amy said, "You were gone for three nights.
We were so worried! They told us they couldn't go out and
search for you."
Henry inquired, "What happened? You made it through the flood;
how did you do it?"

"Through the intermeshing worlds!" she exclaimed,
and drew a line in the sequins with a spiral on either end.
One circled clockwise, the other counterclockwise.
"Is that what you saw out there?" Joe asked.
"It's there for everyone to see," she replied.
Alice laughed and gave her some coffee.

"Oh well, some trip," Geni briefed Amy. "I didn't see anything
I set out to see, but now I know that death is part of life, and
there's something bigger out there, bigger than the things I thought
I wanted. And it connects us all, whether we are dead or alive."

Road out of Town

A DAY LATER, Geni and Amy packed their luggage into the car
to go to the airport. Geni looked through the backpack and found her
inhaler. She tossed it onto the back seat: "There's something I don't
need anymore."

It was just after dawn. They pulled their car out from the parking lot
and drove down Main Street. Geni slammed on the breaks, as a
big tawny house cat strolled leisurely across the road in front of them.
Its oversized tail twitched as it descended into the ditch parallel to
the edge of the road.

Geni announced: "There's another connection: puma cat!

At the Airport

A HUGE mountain chain encased the tarmac of the airport.
Geni and Amy were held fast inside its encircling embrace of endless
glass. Outside, a plane crawled by. Geni could only see its tail fin.
It carried a portrait of a puma with a luminous gaze. Geni laughed out
loud with recognition and nudged Amy's arm. "Look, another puma."

*This is a living actuality. Something of the cat's energy protected and
guided me along the way. Thank you. Thank you.*

She heard the vocal hum of a thousand ancestors and remembered
her cat Durarte, Rosette porcupine, her husband Tom, Ella the camel,
her family, and acquaintances. She sighed.
A lot of life was bearing with suffering, but right now, and later again,
magic would show up too.

When the boarding call sounded the backpack held the image of the
plant stem with the infinity sign through it—except now it was
growing out of a heart. Geni settled down and touched the
jewel inside her pocket.

*I swim in the sea, fly in the sky, crawl over the Earth.
I seek other animals, invite them into my lair;
we dance together in fire modeled Shadows of before.
The tide hisses in the snow, Bubbles on our hips swing out and die,
Their rainbows stick
Cooking new air we breathe.
Phases, ever-changing Moons, breed sustenance.
Awake or in sleep, a song ricochets inside heads;
Sings, booting starlight.*

*We are the animals of the day. We bring the fear, the love,
the pathway thru the gate where we travel,
Sharing or denying the others:
allowing for mystery or demise of possibilities.
Retracting claws, eschewing blood,
I prefer to eat the flowers of suns and drink waters of gold
rippling thru the Never-Ending.*

～

About the Author

LILI WHITE has been exploring origins of myth, primacy of memory, exercises in self and counter self–imagining, and dreaming through her painting, sculpture, and over 100 moving image works.

A graduate of the Pennsylvania Academy of Fine Art's four-year painting study and the University of Pennsylvania; she likes to travel and lives in NYC with her husband.

CAT MOTHER, created during the COVID 19 lockdown, has also been developed into theatre and film scripts.

www.liliwhite.com